NEEDLE

NEEDLE

PATRICE LAWRENCE

Barrington Stoke

First published in 2022 in Great Britain by
Barrington Stoke Ltd
18 Walker Street, Edinburgh, EH3 7LP

www.barringtonstoke.co.uk

A CIP catalogue record for this book is available
from the British Library upon request

ISBN: 978-1-80090-101-8

Printed by Hussar Books, Poland

*To LJ for bringing people together
to change this*

CHAPTER 1

I've got my needles. I've got my wool. And now, I'm gonna knit. Some folks like to pray. Some folks like yoga. My foster mum, Annie – she's one of them yoga people. But me, I knit when I'm stressed out. Today was a big stress out. It's lucky I've got something big to knit. I mean proper big. Dinosaur big.

I don't even like dinosaurs. (Of course I haven't met no dinosaurs face to face. And most of them have faces way too high up for me to see anyway.) But some kids are obsessed with dinosaurs. They know what every dinosaur is called. Their full Latin names and everything. My little sister, Kandi, is one of those kids. I'm knitting something special, just for her.

I haven't seen Kandi for two years now. When our mum died, there wasn't no one around who could look after both of us. Kandi went to live with her dad. But no one knew where my dad had gone and our aunty had baby twins and didn't have room for me.

So I live with Annie. I've been here for ten months now. It's the third place I've lived since me and Kandi got split up. Annie's been fostering kids like me for ages. Her parents used to foster kids too. Me and Annie get on all right. She tells me she's in it for the long term. But sometimes we have to work at our relationship, as she puts it.

Annie runs a yoga studio in an alley off the high street. She says to me, "Charlene, yoga's perfect for slowing down our minds and easing our stress."

Annie's offered me free classes any time I want. But I got my knitting to slow down my mind and help me deal with stress. I don't need to stare at other people's bums for an hour.

Annie's got a son called Blake. He's at uni, so I've got his old room. I know he's not happy with that. He wants it free for when he comes back here. Still, the third bedroom he sleeps in isn't that small. At least he doesn't have to share like me and Kandi did until we got separated.

Last time Blake was here, Annie made him wash his own clothes, the same way I have to. I heard them arguing. Annie said, "*I'm your mother, not your slave, Blake. You know how the washing machine works.*" Blake acted like it was my fault she was making him do this, despite him seeing me unloading my clothes and hanging them out in the garden to dry.

Annie's been helping me with dinosaur research. We went to the library and found a whole load of books with pictures of dinosaurs in them. Then she found some small toy dinosaurs in an old box in a cupboard in the loft. They used to belong to Blake when he was a kid. Last week, me and Annie spent a couple of evenings watching the *Jurassic Park* films. We thought about watching the *Jurassic World* films too but didn't. Annie said that she didn't want to ruin her memory of the originals. And me, like I said, I'm just not that into dinosaurs.

But I want to make sure I get everything right for Kandi. I can't knit a real-size dinosaur. Annie hasn't got a ladder that tall nor pockets that deep to buy all that wool. I'm making my little sister a kind of blanket that she can wrap around herself, with a dinosaur hood to pull over her head. Because, man, do you want to know another one of Kandi's favourite things? It was when we wriggled under the covers to the bottom of her bed. Then I'd use my phone torch to read her favourite dinosaur books. We even kept doing it when she could read them herself.

I miss Kandi so much.

Right now, Annie's downstairs eating dinner. I've told her I'm too stressed and I don't want nothing to eat. She says the food's waiting in the fridge for when I'm ready. I can just stick it in the microwave, but I shouldn't bring it up here to my bedroom. Annie had a foster kid a couple of years ago that stored doughnuts in the wardrobe and the place ended up full of mice.

No food. Just knitting. I need to close my eyes and feel the stitches as they slip from one needle to the other. I need the *click, click, click*.

When you're knitting, there's no silence until you finish it.

Click, click, click.

I hope my heart calms down soon.

Click.

Click.

Click.

If I knit too fast, the stitches are gonna drop and there's gonna be holes. I don't want that. If there's holes, I'll have to start again.

Click.

And it's working – it's slowing me down, even though I don't like the way this cheap wool feels. When I was a kid, I picked up a stone and there was a slug stuck to it. The slug fell into my hand and I screamed. The wool reminds me of that feeling, except it's not wet and slimy. My last social worker, Wanda, bought the wool for me out of her own money before she left and started training to be a teacher. I'm really grateful. I just wish it didn't feel so weird. But this is for Kandi, so I'm gonna make myself use it.

My stomach just rumbled. It's lying. I'm not hungry.

Click, click, click, click, click.

I'm going too fast again. I want my knitting to make me stop thinking about what happened in that shop earlier. It's the thing that stressed me out today. Annie believes my version of the story. She's even cooked macaroni cheese for dinner because she knows it's my favourite. She wants me to feel better. Annie says that no stuck-up security guard from a make-up store is gonna make her feel bad about me. But maybe me swearing didn't help, Annie says. And she reckons it would have been much easier if I'd just said sorry.

Nuh! Why should I have said sorry? That security dude had his eyes on me from the second I walked into that shop. One minute the dude was slouching by the wire baskets; next minute it was like someone pulled a string on the top of his head and he bounced right up. I know me and my friends can be loud, but that proves we've got nothing to hide. We're not sneaking around stashing lipstick in our pockets. All our conversation was in the air for him to hear.

Click, click, click, click, click. Need to slow down. Need to slow down.

I'm gonna let my needles rest until my brain cools a bit. I'm not gonna let that ignorant security guard ruin Kandi's blanket too.

I had twenty pounds to spend. The first thing I was gonna buy in that shop was foundation. When I give Kandi this blanket, I want to look good. I don't want her to worry about me. My skin's a bit grey at the moment and the spots on my nose have been there for so long they should be paying me rent.

Me, Bash and Skye are all different colours, so we needed a shop that has make-up for all of us, but one where an eyeliner doesn't cost more than our trainers. Skye reckoned that the big store near the station called Spruce would be good. Apart from the security guard, it seemed all right at first. A make-up girl was sitting on a stool in front of a table of mirrors. She didn't have no customers. She smiled at us and told us to come and ask if we needed anything.

We tried out all the testers. It was fun. Especially when we tried each other's. We were joking with each other because we're pale, or dark, or midway brown. I could see the make-up girl looking confused. She was probably wondering if she should report us for being racist.

"Chaz! You gonna buy this?" Bash asked.

She showed me a bottle of foundation. No squeezy tube. This was proper glass with a screw lid. I couldn't see "Tester" written on the side, so it was the real product. I took it and shook it. The colour inside was light. It wouldn't even match the inside of my hand.

"Yeah," I said. "Get me that green Crazy Hair Dye and that red lipstick there and I'll cosplay the Joker."

I didn't mean it for real. It was jokes. I like Batman even less than I like dinosaurs. But Bash likes to push things. She grabbed a red lipstick from the tester slot. There was only a short nub of it left, like folks had been sneaking in to touch up their make-up for free.

"You better try it on then, Chaz!" Bash said.

She dived towards me. All l could think about was all the other mouths that lipstick must have touched. Stranger spit and germs all over it.

"Nuh!" I said, and moved to push Bash away. The posh foundation slipped from my hand. The smash as it hit the floor was so loud I was surprised people across the street didn't throw themselves to the ground, thinking it was a bomb.

"Man!" Skye said, looking furious. "See what you done?"

Her new white trainers were splashed with make-up, but you could barely see the difference. That foundation was so damn pale. The floor was darker though. The foundation really showed up and it looked like there was more make-up on the floor than there ever was in the bottle.

"You need to pay for that."

It was the security guard. He was smirking, like he'd been waiting for this to happen. The make-up girl was by his side. Her face said *"Don't worry"*. Her mouth said nothing at all. I looked for Skye and Bash. They were gone.

The thing is, I almost said sorry to the make-up girl. It was an accident, but the bottle slipped from *my* hand and smashed. Maybe the shop was gonna take it out of her wages. But I kept my mouth shut because the security guard came up so close to me I was sure I could smell what he had for lunch. I knew he wanted me to know for sure that he was taller than me.

The security guard said, "Did you hear me? You need to pay for that."

I laughed. Not because of his comic vibes. He didn't have any. It was because I've met loads of bullies like this before. They don't know what to do if you don't act scared. I had money to pay. I might even have got a couple of pennies in change. Still, I sure as hell wasn't giving nothing to him.

I stayed exactly where I was. I knew the guard wanted me to step back and act all timid. I took a quick glance round the shop. Yeah, I was checking for escape routes but also looking for my friends.

I saw Skye. She was pressing her nose against the shop window outside. She grinned and waved like all this was still jokes. Bash wasn't nowhere. Her parents don't like her hanging out with us. They think me and Skye are trouble. When crap like this happens, it's like it proves her parents right.

An older white lady had appeared by my side. "I saw everything!" she said. She was wearing a hot-pink tracksuit and had an owl tattooed on her wrist. I sort of wished she was my social worker. "It was an accident, wasn't it, love?"

I nodded. I didn't dash their posh make-up to the ground on purpose. Anyone could see that.

The security guard hit the white lady with a stink-eye. "So will *you* pay for it, madam?" he asked.

My new friend seemed to make herself taller. Seriously, I'm sure I heard her calf muscles stretch when she was doing it. She and the security guard were eye to eye. I hoped both of them had good spit control or they'd be splattering each other's faces when they talked.

"Don't be ridiculous," the lady said. "You have insurance for that. I'm sure that if I'd dropped it, you wouldn't be so harsh."

A crowd gathered round us. I could see folks looking all confused. The security guard was as Black as me. They couldn't understand why he should be treating me different. But the world doesn't always unroll all smooth. When you're a Black girl in care, there's bumps and twists.

"An accident?" the security guard said, laughing. "She isn't even sorry."

The lady smiled down at me and said, "Of course you are, love, aren't you?"

I looked at her and the waiting crowd. I glanced outside at Skye and down at the pale make-up and smashed glass on the floor. It would be easy. All I had to do was say that word.

"No," I said. "It wasn't my fault and I'm not sorry."

CHAPTER 2

Sleep should have made me feel better. It didn't. It wasn't helpful that my empty stomach was gurgling all night. I even turned my light on at 2.30 this morning and added another three rows to Kandi's blanket. Now it's 7.15 and I just want to stay in bed all day, but Annie's gonna keep on knocking on my door until I get up.

I was thinking about my friendships too. I haven't been here long, so it's not like me and Bash and Skye go back to Nursery, but I thought we were mates. I'm gonna have to talk to Bash about running off and leaving me like that. When we were messaging last night, it was easy to pretend that everything that happened in the shop was a laugh. Bash reckoned she left because she was worried that her parents would find out and ban her from seeing me and Skye. I still think she should have stayed and taken the blame. Instead, I was the one who ended up in the shop manager's office and Annie had to leave work and come over.

But I do love it when Annie turns up in places for me – just to see how folks react. I don't know what they expect my guardian to be like, but a tiny white woman in yoga pants isn't it.

Annie strode into that shop yesterday looking like she could tear it down with her bare hands. She was wearing her posh trainers but stomping like Shrek. Annie told them people that they should feel shame for bullying a child like me. The security guard tried to say something about me not being a child. Annie put him right on that, saying *"A fifteen year old is definitely a child unless you can damn well show me the law that says I'm wrong."*

Annie said loud and clear that I wasn't stealing from them. I wasn't abusing no one. If the security guard wanted to pick a public fight, Annie could direct him to the gym below her yoga studio. He'd find a whole room full of macho body-builders he could choose from. If I hadn't been so stressed, I would have cheered.

Another knock on my bedroom door. I need to forget about that and think about school now.

"Charlene!" Annie calls. "I cannot be late this morning!"

I sigh. I know she had to cancel one of her yoga classes when she came over to the shop yesterday. Maybe I'll knit her a bag for her yoga mat to say sorry. I push off the duvet and make myself sit up.

"I'm coming!" I call back.

I manage a speedy shower and smear way too much edge-control gel across my head. These baby hairs are still gonna be smooth when I'm a grandma. I pull on my school uniform and carefully roll up Kandi's blanket. I stash it in one of Annie's old tote bags along with the extra wool and go downstairs.

Annie puffs out her breath. "At last," she says.

She's laid out breakfast things on the table. Yoghurt, a fresh fruit salad and there's even bread in the toaster. My stomach reminds me that it hasn't seen food since the Twix I had after school yesterday.

"What's in the bag?" Annie asks as I sit down.

"Kandi's blanket," I say.

"Are you planning on taking it to school?"

I fill a bowl with fruit salad and spoon yoghurt over the top of it. I mix it all up together. The kid at the place I used to live before Annie's said I made it look like sick. I got moved from there when I heaped a load of apple on my spoon and flicked it at them. I nod at Annie and put a spoonful of breakfast in my mouth. The juice to dairy to banana balance is just right.

Annie says, "I don't think it's a good idea for you to take pointy things to school today, Charlene."

"You mean my needles?" I say, and lay down my spoon. "What do you think I'm gonna do with them?"

"I think you're going to knit with them," Annie says. "Or that's the intention. But you're not in the best of moods."

I push my bowl away and stand up. "What are you trying to say?" I ask.

"What I am saying, Charlene, is that taking metal knitting needles to school isn't a good idea at the best of times," Annie says. She's using her

16

yoga voice – the one where you're done bending yourself double and need to calm down a bit. "What if you're happily knitting away and some other student pulls your blanket from you? What if you act before you realise?"

"You reckon I'm gonna be violent?" I say.

"No, Charlene, I don't. But I do think there are students who would try really hard to provoke you."

I don't say nothing. I know there are kids like that, but I'm not gonna admit it to Annie.

"Or even worse," Annie says, "someone might steal your needles and do something bad with them. Who do you think might get the blame?"

That hurts, mostly because I know she's right. Anything bad is gonna come right back to me even if it's not my fault.

I drop the tote on the kitchen floor and march out the door. Then I come back in, clear away my breakfast stuff and march out again. Annie looks like she's trying to hide a smile but doesn't say nothing.

*

Bash and Skye are waiting for me by the school gate. Skye says that her older sister used to get stopped by that security guard all the time, even when she *wasn't* nicking stuff. Skye hopes that Annie's gonna get him sacked. Me, I don't tell my friends how much they upset me. I didn't like it when all them people were staring at me and I had to style it out and pretend I didn't care. I don't tell them about the woman in the hot-pink tracksuit who came to help me. How she was all on my side at first until I refused to say sorry. Then her face went as hard as the rest of them.

Bash holds out a box with some cake. It's got bright yellow icing on top and a lump of sugary ginger. Bash knows I love ginger.

"Sorry, hun," Bash says. "But you know what my mum's like."

I don't. I've never been to her house. I've never met her mum. But I take the cake anyway.

Skye puts her arm around me. "At least *I* stayed," she says.

I raise my eyebrows.

"You saw me, Chaz!" Skye says. "Checking through the window."

"Through the window?" Bash snorts. "You almost knocked me over trying to get out so fast!"

"But it's your fault I dropped that posh make-up!" I remind Bash.

She laughs loud. "No one can prove nothing!"

I eat my cake. The icing is too thick and too sweet, but I finish it all. Bash and Skye aren't perfect, but I suppose I'm lucky they decided to be my friends at all.

*

The first lesson today is History. Most subjects are streamed at this school so that all the kids the teachers think are clever are put in the same class. Before I started, Annie showed me the school website. They go on and on about their results. Families move into this area just so their kids can go here. That makes Annie laugh. She says that everyone used to think these ends were a dump, and the kids from the estates still end up squashed into the bottom sets for every subject. And me, I'm squashed down there with them.

I'm used to being in the bottom. It's usually because I "need time to catch up". Teachers don't always realise how hard it is to move around and change school. Even those rich kids with tutors would struggle if they'd been to three different secondary schools before Year 9.

That's one reason I'm glad Kandi went to her dad's. She only had to move school once. The last time I heard from her was six months ago and she said she'd made some friends. Then the social worker said that Kandi lost her old phone and her dad won't let her give me the new number.

Kandi's clever. She'll be all right, but me … It's hard trying to catch up with the school work, but it's even worse working out who wants to be your friend. In most schools, the kids have known each other since Nursery. How the hell am I gonna stand a chance with that? One of my social workers said that I should just let my natural cheeriness shine through. She'd clearly never been the new girl in the middle of Year 9.

But I like History. Of course, none of it's my history, so it's like stories. And they more or less tell the same stories at every school. I know the ending too. In my last school, there were only three other kids who weren't white. Here, we're much more mixed up and most of the white kids are from Poland. Mr Mann, our teacher, makes us discuss what we're learning too. He says we should be able to see different viewpoints and learn from each other.

Today's topic is: Is there ever a right side of history? I even looked up stuff in advance about the Scramble for Africa. It's when countries in Europe cut up Africa and gave bits to each other. Annie helped me find out the info in between hunting down dinosaur pics.

But when I walk into the classroom, there's no Mr Mann. Hell's gonna break loose. We got a supply teacher and I'm already feeling sorry for her.

If I had an older sister, she'd look like this supply teacher. Me and her have got the same hair, skin, nose shape and style. I want to like her. She yells for us all to sit down and get out our books and I'm kind of impressed. That's definitely an older-sister voice – an older sister who's got badass siblings that she needs to keep in line.

I sit down at a table bang in the middle of the classroom. Bendi sits down next to me. His full name's Benedict, but the boy gets angry if you use it. I heard rumours that Bendi got excluded from his last school because he broke the head's office window when she called him Benedict during a detention. I don't mind him. Bendi wears his angry on the outside. I know where I stand.

The teacher says her name is Ms Nzegwu. She writes it on the whiteboard for us.

Charity and Tori make fun of the name, twisting their mouths up around the "z". A Nigerian kid called Josh who joined our class last week starts shouting at them and calling them racist. Bendi sighs. I have to stop myself throwing a few words at Charity and Tori too. I reckon that Annie needs a 24-hour gap before getting another phone call about me.

I take a deep breath. Even though I haven't got my knitting with me, I try to imagine the stitches slipping along the needles, the wool not too tight but not too slack, a T-rex forehead getting bigger and wider.

Click, click, click.

Ms Nzegwu shouts again. There's silence.

"So all of you want to talk about racism?" she says, quietly now.

Ms Nzegwu picks up the globe Mr Mann keeps on his desk and spins it. As it slows down, she says, "Look at the size and shape of those countries."

I want to see. I lean closer, but she doesn't hand the globe round. Maybe she's heard that there are kids in this class who like to throw things.

Ms Nzegwu turns on the whiteboard.

"Now look at these maps of the same countries," she says.

When it's all flattened out, the countries are different sizes compared to what they are on the globe. Ms Nzegwu asks us if it's racist to make some countries look smaller than they are and others much bigger. Can maps ever tell the true story? Does it even matter? If I really had my needles, I'd probably drop a stitch because I'm too busy listening and thinking about what she's saying.

Charity puts up her hand and asks, "If they make China look bigger, doesn't that make it racist against white people?"

"You're so dense – you can't be racist against white people!"

That's Josh. He stands up so fast, his chair falls back. He storms towards Charity. Charity stands up too, her chin stuck out like she wants to dig a hole with it.

Ms Nzegwu looks like she's gonna magic a thunderbolt out of thin air and throw it at them. I feel sorry for her again. No one wants to walk into a class and deal with this. And, man, I don't want to. I just want to learn the history.

I stand up before I realise it. I yell at Josh and Charity. I say a swear word. The door opens and Ms Shaw, the head teacher, walks in. Suddenly, I'm the only student standing up, the only one making noise. Ms Shaw looks from me to Ms Nzegwu.

"What's going on here?" Ms Shaw asks.

I point at Charity and start to say, "She—"

"Charlene, sit down, please," Ms Shaw says.

I do. Annie says I should choose my battles and I'm not gonna go all warrior queen on Ms Shaw just yet. The head fixes her stare on Ms Nzegwu.

"I heard the noise from this classroom from down the corridor," Ms Shaw says.

Ms Nzegwu stares right back. There's no nervous eye drop or nothing. I'm dead proud.

"We were discussing racism," Ms Nzegwu says. "As I'm sure you know, Ms Shaw, it's a subject that often gets heated."

"There's a difference between 'heated' and 'unruly'," Ms Shaw says. Her eye turns towards me again. "What point were *you* making, Charlene?"

Charity makes a strange noise. I know that it's her pretending to hide a laugh but making it loud enough for me to know she's laughing at me. I shouldn't let Charity bother me. Who cares what she thinks? I must do, because the words are coming out of me.

"I was making the point that Charity is ignorant," I say, except I add another swear word in there too.

Bendi gasps. Ms Shaw holds the door open.

"My office. Now," the head says to me.

Just for a second, I lock eyes with Ms Nzegwu. She gives a tiny shake of her head and looks sad.

I put my pencil case and books in my bag. I stand up slowly. I can feel everyone watching me. I nod to Ms Shaw, then I turn around and sweep all of Charity's stuff from the table onto the floor. Her water bottle clangs, rolls towards my feet and stops.

CHAPTER 3

I have to wait in the corridor of shame outside the head's office. Annie can't come for me until after the first break. I don't feel no shame about Charity, but I wish I hadn't mashed up Ms Nzegwu's class like that.

When Annie turns up, she's vexed. Her lips are squeezed together so tight it looks like she's used Skye's eyelash glue on them. I'm not sure yet if it's me or the school that's got Annie in a rage.

Me and Annie spend half an hour in Ms Shaw's office. I know it's that long because there's a small clock on the bookshelf behind her. I stare at it after I give up trying to tell Ms Shaw my side of the story. She just wants to talk about my swearing and, in her words, my "aggressive behaviour".

At least Ms Shaw doesn't turn Charity into any kind of angel, but I know how it must have looked – me tall and dark, standing over little blonde Charity. I reckon the sun even shone around Charity's hair like a halo.

"Of course I'll pay for that girl's water bottle," Annie says. "But surely if it's made of metal, it can't break, can it?"

I stare even harder at the clock so I don't smile. *Thank you, Annie.*

Ms Shaw clunks Charity's water bottle onto her desk.

"There is a dent," she says.

A laugh bubbles out of me. I saw Charity throw that bottle at a Year 11 outside the newsagent's in Cole Street. I bet that's how that dent happened. But Annie and Ms Shaw are both staring at me.

I look back at the clock.

"So what's next?" Annie asks.

"As you know, Ms Morrisey ..." Ms Shaw says to Annie.

Annie nods.

"Behaviour like this ..."

Annie nods again.

"Is an automatic exclusion," Ms Shaw finishes.

Annie leans forward and says, "Really, Ms Shaw? Charlene has just started to settle down here. After all the disruption she's had to deal with, on top of the loss of her mother, do you think time out of school is the best thing for her?"

I appreciate Annie's effort, but I don't think school's ever gonna make me feel better about my mum passing away.

Ms Shaw seems to agree with me. "Charlene agreed to abide by the student code of conduct when she joined us." She stares hard at Annie and adds, "Parents and carers sign the agreement too."

Annie flicks the water bottle. The dent makes the ping sound flat. "And what about Charity?" Annie asks. "Is she getting punished too?"

Ms Shaw turns to me. I see her out of the corner of my eye as I stay focused on the clock face.

"Do you believe Charity should be punished, Charlene?" Ms Shaw asks.

I don't say nothing in case another swear word slips out.

"What did she do to provoke you?" Annie asks.

What am I supposed to say? Charity pretended to laugh? I haven't got enough words to explain it. I've let Charity get under my skin. She's scratching away like an inside-out tattoo.

"So you don't think she should be punished?" Ms Shaw asks.

I give up on the clock and stare Ms Shaw in the eye.

"Yes, Charity should be punished," I say. "Because she's ignorant."

Annie and Ms Shaw sigh at the same time. There's so much air from them I feel my cheek wobble. I wish I'd said what was really in my head – that I like History lessons and I like Ms Nzegwu. I wanted the lesson to go properly.

"Two days' exclusion," Ms Shaw says. "And of course, you'll have to say sorry to Charity."

*

Annie had to get a cab from the yoga studio because she didn't want to lose her parking space, so we have to walk home. Well, it's more of a trot. Annie doesn't know how to walk slow. I try to tell her that I'll be all right to go home by myself, but she's having none of it.

"You're angry, Charlene," Annie says. "I'm not leaving you yet. I've already asked Umbereen to take my next class. She's better with the beginners than I am anyway."

I almost say it then. *"Sorry for causing you stress."*

But then Annie says, "Sometimes you need to hold it down, Charlene. It wasn't easy to get you into that school. I was really hoping you'd make the most of it."

"I am making the most of it," I say.

"By telling Charity to – well, you know exactly what you told her to do."

"Because she's igno—"

"Yes!" Annie cuts me off.

We've reached the house and Annie jabs the key at the lock. She misses.

"Charity is ignorant!" Annie says. "You've made that very clear! But the world's full of ignorant people and you can't swear at all of them!" She stabs the lock again. This time the key slips in.

I run straight upstairs to my bedroom. Annie calls up something about lunch, but I don't answer. I spot the tote bag. Annie must have brought it up here. I pull out my knitting, but the needles won't move smooth. My wool feels like it's full of salt – like my hair when I've been for a swim in the sea. Then I drop a stitch. And another one.

There's a knock on the door. Annie's holding a steaming mug. It's one of her herbal brews, but she knows she's got to add three spoons of sugar if I'm gonna drink it.

Annie places the mug on the coaster she gave me for my birthday because she was fed up of the mug rings on the bedside drawers. She had it made for me specially. It's got my face on it, but it looks like my face has been knitted.

Annie spreads Kandi's blanket across the bed.

"Great work," she says.

I don't say nothing. My throat's tight and I want to pull the knitting out of her hands. Annie's wrong. I want it to be perfect, but now it's got holes.

"Your sister's going to love this," Annie says.

"It's rubbish." I realise I sound like a three year old, but that's how I feel. "It's all mucked up."

Annie looks at it more closely. "Ah. I see your problem." She picks up my needles. "May I?"

I nod. I don't let many people touch my knitting. I learned that the hard way. Some folks turn into kittens and can't help pulling and tugging. But Annie knows what she's doing.

She sits down on the bed, with the knitting in her lap. She gently nudges the tip of the needle under the dropped stitch and lifts it. I watch as it slips back down the needle to join the others. She does it again and again.

"Good as new," Annie says.

"Thank you." It comes out as a whisper, but I know she's heard me.

*

Annie makes me eat lunch. Luckily, there's macaroni cheese left over from yesterday and I'm so ready for it. Annie's even sliced up some of those baby cucumbers that I like because they've actually got flavour. Sweet cucumbers to sweeten me up.

She unloads the dishwasher as she talks to me. We both know that's my chore, but it's easier to have these kinds of conversations if we're not staring at each other across a table.

"I know you think the school's being unfair," Annie says. "But if you could do it this once, Charlene. Say sorry. Make our lives easier."

I push the last slice of cucumber aside. "But I'm not sorry," I say. "I'd be lying."

Annie turns to face me. She has her thinking face on. "What if you start off writing a letter to someone who you ... maybe ... you really think you do owe an apology to?"

I don't reply, but I instantly know who that would be.

"Then maybe when you're in the sorry zone, you can knock off a couple more letters." Annie says this so fast I almost miss it. "Before your brain kicks in and realises what you're up to."

"You want me to trick my head into writing 'sorry-not-really-sorry-letters'?" I say.

"Something like that. Think about it."

Annie kisses me on the cheek before she goes.

I clear away the lunch things and go back upstairs to my room. I don't pick up my knitting straight away. I look in all the books until I find the pictures of the T-rexes and lay them side by side. I think about handing Kandi the finished blanket and watching her unwrap it. She'd grin at me, so happy. Maybe I can even teach her how to knit too. When she's older, Kandi might make something for me.

I tear a blank page out from a workbook from my last school. Annie's bought me a whole load of pens, so I've got a big choice. She says that having all them colours around me might inspire me. I keep the pens in some enamel mugs I bought in the market. I pick up a gold pen, but sometimes it goes a bit blotchy. I want this to be perfect. I choose a greeny-blue that makes me think I'm looking into the bottom of a swimming pool, where everything's cool and still.

I start:

Dear Kandi,

Sorry

Am I really gonna start with "Sorry"? She's my little sister. So, yeah. I owe her the apology.

Dear Kandi,

Sorry I still can't come and see you. The social workers made me move ...

I take a big breath. The words splash onto the page.

The social workers made me move from my first place because I kicked a tin of white paint at my foster dad's shed. He'd only just finished building it. The paint

was for the inside, but it splashed all
over the outside, on the windows and
everything. I did it because my foster dad
wouldn't bring me to see you. I wanted to
be with you for your birthday, but your
dad didn't want me to come. He said that
you get upset when you see me and you
can't stop crying for ages afterwards.
That's why I got cross and kicked the
paint.

Then when I moved to the next place, this
kid teased me about how I ate breakfast
and ...

I'm writing this down and I know it's making me look so bad. But me and Kandi were close, man. The last time we saw each other properly was at Mum's funeral and we didn't know what to say. I told her dad that me and Kandi should never have been split up. I think that's when he asked social services if we could have a "pause" on me seeing her. That's the word Kandi's dad used, like he's watching his favourite film and needs to slip out for a quick pee. Pause.

Annie agrees that me and Kandi should see each other, but she says that we can't always control the world. Sometimes we just have to stand back and work out how to pull it back into a shape that's good for us. That's easier for people like Annie than me. She doesn't have folks always shaping her world for her, then expecting her to smile and say it fits.

I'll go back to the sentence about breakfast later. What else do I want to say?

I know you miss me, Kandi. I miss you and think about you all the time. I'm making something really special for you. Annie's promised that we can meet up soon so I can give it to you.

I love you to the moon and back.
Chay Chay xxxxxxx

I sign it big so she can't miss that it's from me. Annie has to see it first before I send it. Then she'll tell Kandi's dad that it's on its way or he'll send it back unopened. I'm glad that Annie is honest with me about these things, but sometimes

I wish that I didn't know. They sit inside my head for too long and prickle.

I tear out another blank page. Am I in the sorry zone? I think of Ms Nzegwu and her sad face. I didn't mean to get her in trouble with Ms Shaw, though it wasn't all my fault. Maybe I can apologise to Ms Nzegwu next. I try writing a few words. I say that I'm sorry that things went wrong. I was really interested in what she was saying and I wanted to have the debate. I say that I hope everything went OK later. I sign my name and put the letter aside.

And now it's time for Charity. *Sorry zone. Sorry zone.* I want to get my brain into it, but it's like trying to push an elephant into a mouse hole.

Dear Charity,

She's not "dear". I cross it out. Then I cross out "Charity". I don't want to say her name, not even with a pen. It's all a splodgy mess now, so I have to tear out another sheet of paper.

I stare at it. Then I start.

I'm sorry you're so ignorant. You don't know nothing, but you always have to open your big mouth. I know you do it just to annoy me and it works! I should stay quiet and ...

And that's it. There's no more I want to say. I cross out "and" and add a full stop – it's a blotch not a dot. I write my name below. Big capital letters. I want to make sure that Charity knows it's from me too.

Annie keeps a pack of envelopes in the drawers in the small room next to the kitchen. As I come downstairs, my heart almost stops. There's a man in the hallway. He turns round to face me. It's Annie's son, Blake.

He frowns. "Shouldn't you be at school?" Blake asks.

I carry on down the stairs. "Shouldn't you be at uni?" I say.

"Tomorrow's lecture is cancelled. I thought I'd make a long weekend of it – see my mum and stuff. What's your excuse?"

I don't say nothing.

Blake nods. "Oh. I get it. You've got thrown out of school again."

I follow him into the small room. It leads to the kitchen. Blake opens the fridge and closes it again, sighing loudly to make sure I hear it.

"I hate macaroni cheese," Blake says. "Isn't there anything else?"

"Look in the freezer," I say.

I don't need to tell him where to find food. He's making a point. Blake wants food prepared for him in the fridge at all times just in case he's passing by.

Blake shrugs and says, "I'll get take-out."

He pushes back past me, grabs his rucksack from the hallway and thunders upstairs. I dig through the small chest of drawers and find the envelopes in the bottom one, hidden beneath some tea towels. I grab a handful of envelopes and take them back up.

I stop by my bedroom doorway. I can't go further. Blake's in my room. He's standing by my bed holding up my letter to Charity. He has no right to be in my room. He has no right to touch my letter. Annie told me from the beginning that this room is my personal space and she will respect that. Even she knocks. I think of the security guard and how he stood so close to me to make me feel small. I know why Blake's really in here. It's to remind me that this is *his* room in *his* house.

I take a deep breath. I don't care about Charity, but I care about Ms Nzegwu. I probably made things bad for her. I don't care about Blake, but I do care about Annie. I don't want to make things bad for her too.

I make myself look at Blake's hand holding my letter. His thumb and finger are holding it tight like it's the brakes on a bike. Another deep breath.

My head clears a bit. I don't mind Blake reading my letter to Charity. It's nothing private. But my letter to Kandi is right there, next to my knitting. It's face down, so Blake can't see the writing. I try not to look at it, because he's staring at me with a smirk.

"Why d'you have to write this?" Blake asks.

"None of your business," I say.

I want to take the words straight back and say something calmer. It's like my brain plans one thing and my mouth says something different.

"I reckon it is my business," Blake says. "Because if you've got thrown out of school and you've got to write this." He waves the letter. "Then that's going to stress Mum."

The breeze from the window moves Kandi's letter across the bed. The wind nudges a ball of brown wool. Blake looks down at it. I clench my fists behind my back and force my face to stay neutral.

"You done?" I say. "Because you're not supposed to be in here, right?"

Blake glances down at Kandi's letter. I'm proud of myself. I don't even twitch, but behind my back I'm squeezing my thumbs into porridge. Blake lets Charity's letter flutter from his hand. Then he reaches down and prods my knitting.

"What's this?" Blake asks.

"Leave it alone, Blake," I say.

"I'm only asking. Mum says I should get to know you properly. She says you're really lovely under the bravado."

I blush. Lucky, with my skin colour he doesn't know. It's not embarrassment, just crossness. What sort of conversations does Annie have with her son about me when I'm not there?

Blake pokes a ball of wool. His fingernail catches and a tiny thread pulls loose. I swallow hard, imagining my anger pressed flat in my throat.

"Mum says you're brilliant at knitting," Blake says. "She reckons you can make anything."

I force out a smile. I even manage to hold it when Blake picks up Kandi's blanket. He's careful, making sure the needles don't slip out. He squints at it.

"This a T-rex?" He sounds impressed.

I nod.

"Who's it for?" Blake asks.

I could lie, but I just want the questions to be over. I want Blake to put down my knitting and leave the room. Then I'll close the door and sit with my back against it and not move again until Annie's home.

"My sister," I say.

"I heard you're not allowed to see her."

Annie had no right to tell Blake that! Man, she's letting my trust leak right through her.

I say, "That's none of your business neither."

Blake shrugs and says, "I suppose not." He holds my knitting up close to his face. His breath's twisting through the wool. "But this is good."

"I know."

That's not the proper way to accept a compliment. I know that. You're supposed to smile politely. You're supposed to say thank you politely. You're supposed to change the conversation or pretend you're not really *that* good. Why? Seriously, why? I am a damn good knitter and I'm not gonna pretend otherwise.

Blake says, "Do you take commissions?"

He's still holding my knitting. His talk sounds friendly, but I can see how he's watching me.

"What?" I say.

"Commissions." Blake lays the knitting down and for a second I can breathe. Then he grabs a needle in each hand and holds them wide apart, stretching the blanket tight between them. It doesn't look like a dinosaur any more, just patches of colour.

"Put it down, Blake," I say.

"Commissions are when you get paid for doing something," Blake tells me.

I'm sure I can hear the wool stretch, the tension pulling tighter.

"I know what 'commissions' mean," I reply.

"You've got a good eye," Blake says. "Proper talent. I could ask you to ... knit ... Sherlock Holmes." He grins.

"Why the hell should I knit Sherlock Holmes?"

Why the hell don't I just dive at him and grab my knitting back? Or yell at him that he shouldn't be in my bedroom at all? Because I know that's what he wants me to do.

"Because I can pay you," Blake says.

I don't need his money. I don't want it.

"Gina's obsessed with *Sherlock*," Blake carries on. Gina's his girlfriend. "It's her birthday next month and I promised her something special. Can you knit Benedict Cumberbatch as Sherlock Holmes?"

I've just got to agree. Then he'll put Kandi's blanket down. He'll go away.

I say, "Yeah. But you'll have to buy the wool."

The doorbell rings. We don't move.

"I'm not expecting anyone," Blake says. "Are you?"

I bought some second-hand boots off Depop last week. This could be them at last.

"You better hurry up," Blake says. "If it's for you, they'll leave a note and then it'll take ages to hunt your stuff down."

Another doorbell ring – longer this time. Blake raises his eyebrows. He's still holding my knitting.

My heart's beating and I'm working so hard now to keep my face blank. I turn around slowly and walk out the bedroom door, then race down the stairs.

I pull the front door open so fast, the delivery man's almost swept into the hallway. The parcel he's holding – maybe it could hold bootees but never boots. It's only slightly too big to fit into the letterbox. And, man, it's not even for our house – it's for the Nigerian woman who lives three doors away. The delivery man takes my name and a picture of the parcel in the doorway. I close the front door again and run back upstairs.

Blake's left the bedroom. He's left the bedroom and taken my knitting. It's nowhere to be seen, but Kandi's letter's been turned over. I can see the writing facing up now. My heart's beating so hard, I can feel it in my throat, behind my eyes, even in my fingertips.

"Blake!" I shout.

I storm along the hallway and throw open his door. There's no Blake, but I see my needles, thrown on the rug by the bed. They've fallen in a cross shape like I should find treasure beneath them. Then I see my knitting all separate. But it's mostly not knitting – it's a tangle spread across the bed.

I bend down and pick up the needles. My fingers feel thick and heavy, like they could never hold anything delicate no more without breaking it.

"Well, you said you needed wool," Blake says.

He's standing in the doorway. He's grinning. And he's waiting.

I can knit it back. If I did it once, I can do it again. And next time it'll be better. Yeah, this is just a practice run and ...

Telling myself this doesn't work. My brain knows better. My brain knows that I poured all my love into this blanket. Love was knitted into every stitch so that Kandi could feel it when she held it close to her. I can't do it again. Not like this.

"So are you going to do me Sherlock Holmes then?" Blake says.

I look at him standing there grinning with one hand resting against the door frame. Something inside me bursts and it pushes me towards him. I think I'm crying. I know I'm holding the needles. Then I hear Blake shriek and I see the blood.

CHAPTER 4

I call the ambulance. No one will remember that, but it was me. Noreen who lives next door heard Blake scream and called the police as well.

They turn up quick. The police cars have even got their sirens on. All the street must be having a look. Blake opens the door to the feds. He's wrapped his hand in the tea towel I bought Annie as a prezzie on a school trip to Brighton. Now there's blood all over the Brighton Pavilion and the domes are smeared brown and red.

There's one policeman, one policewoman, but I see there's a tough-looking fed leaning against the car outside and a second police car parked behind it. I don't know what Noreen said when she called them, but, man, she must have made it sound serious.

I watch the way the feds come through the door. I think they're wearing stab vests. They look around at me, at Blake, at the blood on his hand.

Straight away, Blake yells, "That psycho! She stabbed me!"

The feds both look at me. I look down at the floor. I don't want police reading things into my face that aren't true.

"She stabbed me with her knitting needle!" Blake shouts. "It's upstairs."

The policeman takes Blake into the sitting room. The policewoman leads me through the small room into the kitchen. She suggests that we both sit down. She tells me her name and asks me mine. I don't say nothing. I'm not being rude. I'm just tired. It's like there's a tap on the back of my spine and all my energy's pouring out of it. I'm trying to save a bit of energy just to think.

The fed's asking me what happened. And if I'm all right and if ...

I close my eyes, because even looking at her is draining me. I push my chin into my hands and my elbow into the table and try not to cry.

Annie comes home. I hear her voice in the hallway, loud and confident. Annie asks about Blake, then she asks about me. She comes into the kitchen and I want to open my eyes, but now I'm too tired to even do that. Annie tells me she's taking Blake to the hospital. I wonder if he's still got the tea towel wrapped around his hand. Annie will have to leave it at the hospital. It's too nasty to bring home.

Home. Annie's home. Blake's home. Not mine, because I know what's gonna happen next.

"We need to take you to the police station," the fed says.

I force myself to open my eyes and stand up. I look through the small room to the hallway. Annie's opening the front door and Blake has his back to me.

I want to yell at Blake, "*You've got your old room back! Happy now?*"

I *do* yell, "Happy now?"

Annie looks at me, then away again.

*

I go upstairs to pack some things because I know how this works.

The policewoman comes with me. Maybe she's worried that I'm gonna escape through a window or something. She stands in the doorway trying to make polite conversation, but I don't answer. All I can think about is that I'm not coming back here.

I don't want no one else packing my stuff. Last time, I had to throw away eight balls of yarn because they were all shoved together in a plastic bag and got knotted. This time, I leave the wool. What's the point? I'm not gonna see Kandi any time soon. Maybe not ever again. Because I did it. I stabbed Blake. The needle was in my hand and I brought it down fast and hard. Blake was screaming and swearing. The needle stayed there, balancing in the skin between his finger and thumb before he pulled it out. I wanted to throw up. I wanted to cry. But I called for an ambulance instead.

I go with the policewoman to the car. The other car's gone already. She and her police mate chat to each other in the front as they're driving. The radio cuts in and out. I close my eyes again and let it all mix up. The sounds are like different colour wool knotted up and tangled together. I open my eyes and grab the seat and try to make my head as empty as I can.

*

The police station is smaller than the ones I've been in before. It's not my first time. But I've never done anything really bad and sometimes I've just been on the scene.

I was with this girl Jodie when she scraped her key along some teacher's car. I didn't even go to Jodie's school, but watching her made me feel better. I've had a few crap teachers and I've got excluded just for talking back to them. If Jodie was gonna be chucked out of school, I reckoned at least she'd have done something to make it worth it.

Jodie did get chucked out. Then I ended up in the police station because the school had CCTV of me in the car park. It seemed that Jodie had been busy with her key for a few months. The school wanted to catch the culprit and the one time I was with her, that's when our pictures got taken. My social worker said I should say sorry to the teacher, but why? All I did was laugh.

The custody officer's called Elena. It's weird because her voice is like mine – kinda London with other places in it. She's white, but I don't think she was born in the UK. She asks me about an "appropriate adult". I'm still a kid, so someone's got to be with me when they ask me questions.

"Is there someone you would like me to call, Charlene?" Elena asks.

I open my mouth to say, "Annie," and suddenly my stomach feels like it's swelling up. All my feelings have hidden themselves in there and have got so big they want to explode out. I put my hand over my mouth.

Elena the custody officer steps back. "Are you OK?" she asks.

I let my hand drop away. "It's all right. I'm not gonna puke all over your police station."

She says, "If you're feeling ill, we can arrange for someone to come and see you."

I shake my head. I can't tell her that I'm angry at myself.

"So just to be clear," Elena says. "You don't need to see a doctor or anything?"

"No. Thank you," I say.

Elena gives me a small smile. Annie kept saying that a little politeness goes a long way. I bet she didn't realise that I was listening to her. It definitely works on Elena.

"Do you need anything to eat or drink?" Elena asks.

I shake my head.

"And an appropriate adult ...?" Elena asks again.

I shrug.

Elena sighs. "Shall I call social services?"

It's like I have it stitched into my forehead. *This one ain't got no parents who are gonna come for her.*

"There's my aunty," I say. "She lives in Ealing."

When you're in care, folks think it's because you haven't got no one, no family at all. But I got Aunty Jasmine. I always wanted Aunty Jasmine to be my mum, even when my mum was alive. Aunty Jasmine was the one who took me to the cinema and for ice cream in the park and for walks by the river. Once, she took me for a walk by the Thames when my mum was stressed because I kept getting hair nits. The tide was out and it was the first time I'd seen the sand and stones on the river shore. Aunty Jasmine told me that there are people called mudlarks who search for old things there. She stroked my head.

"And you know what, Charlene?" Aunty Jasmine said. *"A mudlark found a nit comb that goes right back to Roman times. Folks have been fighting nits for thousands of years, but the damn mites still get the better of us every time."*

I'd imagined a little Roman kid sitting between their aunty's knees as she combed old-style Roman nit lotion into their hair. And it did make me smile.

Elena nods. "Give me your aunty's details and we'll call her."

Then Elena says they have to put me in a cell. I thought you had to do something proper wrong for the feds to do that. Or be drunk or out your head on drugs. I want to tell them that I don't want to be locked up. Man, I really don't want to. But if I open my mouth to speak, all I'm gonna do is cry.

I've met other kids who spin out the stories about their cell time. It was like they'd been watching old *Law and Order* reruns and they thought they were in New York instead of England. There ain't no tattooed gang boys in here. It just stinks and I can hear someone puking their guts out.

I can't answer when they ask me if I want food or water. My mouth's too dry to talk. My hands feel like they need their knitting needles. I sit on my hands so they press into the thin mattress.

I wait.

*

I don't know how long I wait for. They don't put clocks in police cells. I go up to the door and yell through the hatch, "You calling Aunty Jasmine?"

I wait some more. Then Elena comes up to the hatch.

"I'm afraid your aunty Jasmine can't come," Elena says. She even sounds sad for me. "She's very sorry, but the twins are poorly and there's no one else who can look after them. We're just trying the duty social worker now."

And then Elena goes again. The puking sound stops and I just hear crying.

My fingers are moving. It's like I've got invisible needles and the wool's going slack, then tight, looping and falling. But in truth, I'm just knitting air.

Then I hear the cell door unlocking and Elena opens it up. My legs are wobbly when I stand, but I make my face look hard.

Elena says, "We've found someone for you. The lawyer's arrived too."

She smiles at me like I should be happy at the news.

Elena takes me to an interview room. The duty solicitor's waiting for me there. He's called Roberto. He tells me his name and who he is straight away, maybe in case I think he's a social worker. *Roberto, man, no social worker ever comes into a police station looking like they've walked out a wedding.*

Roberto is wearing a grey suit, white shirt and shiny grey tie. I don't reckon he's much older than Blake. He's kinda got a look of Blake about him too. Same light brown hair, same small ears, same tightness around his shoulders as if he'll throw a tantrum if some foster kid takes his bedroom.

Just then, the door opens. Elena shows in a Black version of Annie – same age and same clothes sense. She's wearing a dark red dress and trainers and has long grey braids pulled back with a scrunchy. A big chain round her neck spells "No-To-Cuts". She and the lawyer look at each other. They don't shake hands.

"Hello, Charlene," she says. "My name's Vera. I'm here as your appropriate adult."

Man, all these names I'm supposed to remember.

I can't get comfortable in the interview room yet. First they've got to book me in. Vera goes with me. This new room is bright and white and the feds are wearing aprons. It's like they use this place for brain operations. I imagine coming out of here with my skull flapping open and an empty hole inside. I want to laugh, but it's not funny. I just feel sick.

I have to open my mouth so they can swab out my cheek for DNA.

I have to let them take my photo. Left. Right. Front. Like they're gonna slap it on some damn Wanted poster and stick it on walls around town.

I have to let them take my fingerprints. Every damn finger, one at a time. Press them against the pad that takes a picture for the computer. It's gonna be like a Police Google now. Tap in my name and see my lovely face and read what they brought me in for today.

Vera's saying sorry that this has to happen to me. She says it's an outrage. But it still happens.

We go back to the interview room. As I sit down opposite Roberto, I get a look at his shoes. They're lace-ups, black, though the toes are a bit worn. I almost like Roberto for that. Maybe he's only got one pair of good shoes and he has to wear them so much they've got old.

Roberto and Elena the custody officer smile at each other.

"Take you away from something, Bob?" she asks Roberto.

"Dinner with the future in-laws." Roberto laughs. "You rescued me!"

Elena laughs too. "Need a coffee?" she asks.

"Please," Roberto replies.

Elena doesn't ask me if I need anything this time.

Elena leaves the room and Roberto turns to Vera.

"Will you be leaving?" he says to her.

Leaving? Why is Vera leaving? She's only just got here.

"Sorry, Charlene," Vera says. "This is your private time with Roberto."

"I don't want private time with Roberto," I say.

Roberto looks annoyed. "Everything you say to *me* is confidential. Do you know what that means?"

Seriously? Sometimes I think my name is really Confidential instead of Charlene, because I hear that word so much. Everything I say is supposed to be confidential, but somehow everyone still seems to know my business.

I nod and say, "I'm familiar with the word."

"Er, good," Roberto says. "Vera isn't allowed to keep what you say confidential. If she stays, the law says that she can be asked about what you say to me. She might even be called to court to answer questions about what we talked about here."

I look from Roberto to Vera.

"So I'm supposed to trust you and not her?" I say.

Roberto looks like he's trying not to grit his teeth together.

He says, "I just want to reassure you that everything we say in here stays in here."

You sure, Bob? You and Elena look like you have a few cosy chats. She doesn't even need to ask you how you like your coffee.

Roberto gives me a smile. I don't smile back. I'm sure as hell not feeling happy right now. He takes a pen and notepad out of a posh-looking satchel.

"I want Vera to stay," I say.

"I don't think that's a good idea," Roberto says.

"I do," I say. I smile at Vera. "I understand that you can't keep what you hear now a secret, but it doesn't matter. I'll be telling Roberto nothing but the truth."

Roberto looks like he wants to say something else but stops himself. Vera sits down again.

"Would you like to tell me what happened, Charlene?" Roberto says.

"What happened when?" I ask.

Roberto gives me a long look. It's the one teachers give you when they're trying to work out if you don't understand what they're saying or just don't care.

"What happened to bring you here?" Roberto says slowly.

His pen's waiting like it's my words that give it power. I wish there was something I could tug in my head so that the story just unravels into one long thread. Instead, it's just loops.

Blake's holding my knitting.

The doorbell rings.

*I go into Blake's room and I see
the tangle of wool.*

I pick up the knitting needle.

I stab Blake's hand.

Blake's holding my knitting.

The doorbell rings.

*I go into Blake's room and I see
the tangle of wool.*

I pick up the knitting needle.

I stab Blake's hand.

My fingers are knitting air again. I still don't
know what to start saying, so Roberto tries to use
his words instead.

"Mr Morrisey alleges that you attacked him
with knitting needles." Roberto's pen moves
across his notepad even though he's only writing
down what he's said himself.

"Don't worry," Roberto says. "I'm here to
make sure you're OK. I'm on your side."

My side? Man's only just met me and I can see by the way he looks at me that he's already formed his opinions. I know whose side he's on.

"It's your chance to tell us your version of events," Roberto says.

Us. He doesn't say "me". He says "us". Roberto and Elena and the rest of the police – in it together.

Vera leans forward and says, "Thank you for reassuring *your* client that you are acting for her and not the police."

Vera moves her chair. She manages to twist her shoulder so it faces Roberto. I can just see his face behind her. He looks annoyed.

"You are his client," Vera says. "*He* has to do what you instruct him to." She says "he" so sharp it makes my teeth ache. "Sometimes lawyers forget that."

Roberto sighs. "Shall we return to the incident?" he asks.

Vera's still facing me as she says, "Is there anything you want to say privately first, Charlene?"

I shake my head. I don't want to say nothing to no one. I don't want to go back into the loop.

Blake's holding my knitting.

The doorbell rings.

I go into Blake's room ...

"What happened today?" Vera asks.

"Mr Morrisey alleges ..." Roberto says, nodding towards me, "that my client attacked him with knitting needles in his bedroom."

"Does he indeed?" Vera says, and touches my arm. "Are you sure there's nothing you want to talk about in private, Charlene? It's important that the police have the full story. Your story. And I know some things can be hard to say."

I look at the desk and my fingers.

Vera says quietly, "Did Blake do something that made you angry?"

I clear my throat. This woman is going to stare at me until I say something.

"I was knitting something for my little sister's birthday," I say. "Blake pulled it apart."

"Knitting," Roberto repeats, scribbling it on his pad. "You enjoy knitting?"

"Why would I do it if I didn't enjoy it?" I say.

Roberto scribbles something else. Maybe "enjoying".

"Of course," he says. "Do you think ... is it something you can knit again?"

"No!" I try not to shout. "It was for my sister! It was special!"

There's silence. I expect Elena to come in with more feds to see what's going on. Roberto's phone vibrates. He glances at it, makes a face, then turns it face down.

"Who taught you to knit?" Vera asks me gently. "I see lots of young people knitting and I always wonder how they learned." She clenches and unclenches her fists. "I'm too clumsy to do anything delicate like that."

"My aunty Jasmine. She started me with big needles," I say. "All I could do was squares. But they weren't really squares because I couldn't get the tension right. But it didn't matter. I used to sit in bed making piles of them until I heard Mum come home."

I see Roberto glance at his watch.

"How old were you?" Vera asks.

"Six," I say. "Or seven."

Vera smiles and says, "You're a seasoned knitter then. You should take commissions."

Commissions? Maybe "Mr Morrisey" missed out that part of the story – how Blake offered me a commission before pulling my blanket apart? I push my chair away from the table and fold my arms. Roberto lays his hand across his pen as if I'm gonna grab it and stab him too. There's silence.

"The police will want to start the interview soon," Roberto says, and glares at Vera. "We better skip ahead to today's events in case we run out of time."

"We'll take as long as we need," Vera says.

Elena brings Roberto's coffee.

She's about to leave when Vera says, "Aren't you going to check if Charlene needs anything?"

Vera turns to me. "Do you want a hot drink or some water?"

"May I have a cup of tea, please?" I don't really want one, but I'm looking at Roberto. He taps his notebook gently and doesn't meet my eye. But Roberto and Elena swap a look. I don't know why people do this and not expect you to notice. Maybe they think they blink into another dimension for half a second.

"A cup of tea, please," Vera says, smiling at Elena.

"Sure," Elena says. "Will you be ready soon?"

Roberto nods.

"I'll let you know," Vera says.

In the end, we *are* ready soon. I tell them my version. It's basics though. They don't need to know nothing extra about me. Why should I tell them that I'm no good at art and I can't spell very well, but I can look at something and work out how to make it in wool? Or how I kicked the white paint across the shed to stop myself crying when I couldn't see Kandi?

"So you admit to stabbing Mr Morrisey?" Roberto says.

Mr Morrisey? Like I'm ever gonna call Blake "Mr".

"Stabbing is an emotive word," Vera says.

"It's the word she – my client – used herself," Roberto replies.

Vera leans forward again as she says, "Which makes it sound like grievous bodily harm. It was just his hand."

"A knitting needle being stabbed through a hand could be considered grievous," Roberto says.

"It wasn't through his hand!" Vera shouts. "It was the skin between his thumb and finger!"

"His right hand! Mr Morrisey is right-handed!" Roberto stretches his hand out and wiggles his thumb. "There could be potential damage to a nerve. Or even to a tendon."

"Worst-case scenario," Vera says. "You are not here to make matters worse."

I close my eyes and let them carry on with their word battle. I think of Blake grabbing the tea towel and wrapping it round his hand. I remember all the names he called me before the police came. He yelled that the damage better not be permanent or I'd be sorry. Then I remember Annie turning round to look at me before she helped Blake out the door. Just a look. No words. "Mr Morrisey" called me a psycho. Even my damn lawyer seems to agree with him.

I don't say nothing else until the interview starts. Then I tell them, "I stabbed Blake in the hand with my knitting needle. And no, I'm not sorry."

CHAPTER 5

Emergency foster place! Here I am! Charlene's in the house for one night only! There's no need to get comfortable. The foster carer's called ... Man, my head's too mashed to remember.

The foster carer is used to kids like me. She even has spare PJs in my size. She actually opened a drawer in the bedroom where I'm staying and told me to take my pick. The drawer was full of pyjamas, all sizes and colours. She offered me a sandwich and a drink and time to chill and a listening ear if I needed it. I took the sandwich and hot chocolate and closed the bedroom door. I didn't mean to be rude. I did say thank you. *See, Annie? I listened to you, right?*

I don't change into the PJs. I don't even take them out the plastic. I think about how vexed Annie would be. She's always going on about how the whole world's wrapped in plastic "and it's SO unnecessary, Charlene".

I don't suppose I'm ever gonna see Annie again. Social services like you to make a clean break. It's like the Lidl middle bargain aisle. Once you're gone, you're gone. But I suppose Annie's gonna be there if this thing goes to court. Of course, she's gonna be on Blake's side, not mine.

I've been Released Under Investigation. Vera said that was probably a good result. Roberto too, before he hurried back to his in-laws. It means the police want more information about what happened before they decide what to do.

I don't know what else they want to find out. All they got to do is go to Annie's and see the tangled-up wool on Blake's bed. Go to my old room and find all those dinosaur books. Maybe they'd understand then. This wasn't just about the blanket. This was about Kandi and me. It still is. Blake did what he did. I did what I did. Now there's no way in hell that Kandi's dad will let me see her again.

I sit on the bed and I can smell the cleanness, like the covers just rolled out of the washing machine onto the duvet. It's not even eight o'clock yet, but it's November. It's been dark for hours.

The foster carer knocks on the door and calls my name. It's faster to answer because she's gonna come in anyway. She's been told I'm upset and has to keep an eye on me. She stands by the door and asks if I want her to turn on the light. I don't. She asks if there's anything I need. I shake my head. She pauses a little longer. She sighs. A sigh plus the way she's standing plus the look on her face tells me what she's gonna say next. *"It's none of my business, but ..."*

"It's none of my business," the foster carer says, "but I just wanted to ..."

She makes an awkward face. She wants to give me advice.

"It's not exactly advice," she says, "but ..."

I think she's waiting for a sign from me. I'm not gonna say nothing, but I raise my eyebrows, just in case she's got good night-time vision and can see them.

"I don't know exactly what happened today," she says. "And of course you don't have to tell me."

Nope.

"But you've been released under investigation, so perhaps it's something less serious?"

Another pause. Maybe the foster carer's waiting for another sign. I know she wants to come and sit on the edge of the bed and give me her advice up close. She needn't bother. I know what's coming next.

"It's just … Charlene, no one wants to get drawn into the court system if they can help it." She sighs again. "I know that from experience."

I'm supposed to ask, "What experience?" But I'm too tired to want to know right now.

"The police might give you a youth caution," the carer says. "If you admit you did it."

I did admit it.

"And they might set up a meeting for you to apologise to the other person."

I look out of the window. The sky looks like dark grey wool with patches of white for the street lights.

"I'm not saying sorry to no one," I say.

"*It's up to you then*." The foster carer doesn't say this, but I hear it in my head like the air said it instead.

"OK, Charlene," she says. "I'm going to have a quick bath, unless you want to go first."

"I'm fine," I say. "I'll have a shower later." Then I ask, "Have you heard how Blake's doing?"

She looks a bit surprised. Even in the shadows I can see her face soften. I want to laugh. She thinks that actually I am sorry. I'm not. I just need to know if there's permanent damage to Blake's hand. That's gonna help decide what happens next.

"No news yet," she says, "but I'll let you know when I hear."

I nod and smile. "Thank you," I say.

She nods back and closes the door gently.

I stay there for a while looking out onto the street. My brain's all muffled up. When I'm knitting, it's like the stress is unwinding itself from inside my head. Now I can't think properly.

I should slip myself between those clean covers and try to sleep. I need my energy for tomorrow, when I find out where I'm gonna live next. But who knows how long I'll even stay there? This time next year I could be in prison.

I can see Blake in court right now. Nice, neat white boy. Hair combed all smooth. Smart suit like Roberto's. Telling the judge how he gave up his bedroom for the poor foster girl. How he's been working so hard at university. How, yes, he did mash up her knitting, but was it worth this? He holds up his hand. Now it hurts when he tries to write his essays. He can't even open jars, or tie up his trainer laces – because he's on his uni's athletics team too. Of course he is.

And me? What are they gonna see when they look at me? Some folks always thought I was heading to prison. I bet they'd be happy to know they're right.

I messaged Skye and Bash when I was in the car coming over here. I needed to tell someone what was going on. Then I ran out of battery. Phone's charged now, but they haven't answered. Bash's mum is probably throwing a "Charlene's Gone" party to celebrate the fact that I'm out of her daughter's life.

I watch a man walking his dog on the other side of the street. The dog's tiny. A squirrel's gonna fight it and win. The dog hasn't got no lead, so it runs ahead, then waits for him. The man's on his phone and it's like the dog just wants him to stop chatting and get the walk done. Suddenly the dog must have had enough and it barks and runs off. The man shoves his phone in his pocket and runs after it.

I rest my head against the window. I don't know if the curtain's damp from my sweat or the condensation on the glass. My brain's still muffled. My thoughts feel like dropped stitches.

Click, click, click.

I try to imagine knitting, but it hurts. All I can see is the ruined T-rex blanket.

My phone buzzes. It's a message from Skye asking me how I am. I see that Bash isn't part of the chat no more. I call Skye. We don't normally talk this way, but I want to hear the voice of someone I know. She's at a barbecue at her sister's and there's people laughing around her. Skye says that if I was nearer, I could come over. Man, Skye, it wouldn't be that easy for someone like me even if I was nearer. Social services don't want us hanging out in strangers' homes.

I tell her about Kandi. It's the first time I've even mentioned I got a sister. It's even the first time I've told her that my mum died. I usually don't tell anyone that. It's too much stress dealing with other people's reactions. You see their faces change and they kind of look embarrassed and then they almost start edging away. But Skye's good. She's had all sorts of stuff happen in her family. One of her little cousins even went into foster care for a while until his mum stopped using drugs.

"Look at it this way, Chaz," Skye says. "You can't do nothing about what the police decide now, especially as that wasteman Blake's gonna do his best to make sure you get locked up."

My stomach hurts. Skye talking about me being locked up makes it feel more real.

"But it doesn't mean that you can't see your sister," Skye says.

"Her dad said—" I start to say.

"And what?" Skye cuts me off. "Who cares what he says?"

Someone at the barbecue calls out that the chicken's ready at last. Someone else shouts that they hope they don't get food poisoning. There's more laughing.

"Last time, Nana bit into a wing and it started bleeding," Skye says. "Look, I got to go or there won't be nothing left for me, but, man, do you have to do what Kandi's dad says? He shouldn't have split you and Kandi up. Go and see her, Chaz. You hear me?"

"Yeah," I say.

"Gonna meet up soon?" Skye asks.

"Yeah."

And then there's no Skye and no barbecue. It's just me sitting here by myself next to the window. It's as easy for Skye to tell me to go and see Kandi as it is for her to invite me to her sister's barbecue. She doesn't know about all the rules I've got to follow.

But, man, do I have to follow them?

I sit upright. I think of that little dog just now that barked and ran away when its owner wouldn't behave properly. The dog decided that it had been patient long enough and was gonna do things its own way. Why can't I?

I tried to follow the rules. I even listened to Annie and wrote those letters, but that didn't get me nowhere. My stomach bubbles. In the school before last, a teacher told us it's adrenalin. It squirts out from glands above our kidneys when we're in danger. We can fight or we can run away. We can run away ...

Who knows where they're gonna take me tomorrow? At least I'm still in the same city as Kandi. I can get to her even if I don't have nothing to take her now. All the hate I've got for Blake makes me feel like I'm plugged into the sun. There's this power zapping inside me and I know it for sure. I have to go to Kandi.

I slide off the bed and open the bedroom door. I peer along the landing. The bathroom door is still shut and I can see light underneath it. The foster carer's got her music playing in there too. If I'm gonna run for it ... Am I gonna run for it? Yeah. I am. I have to do it now.

I go back into the bedroom, pick up my trainers, creep down the stairs and that's it. I'm out the front door. I want to run, but a casual walk is better. Anyone looking out their window's gonna remember a stressed girl sprinting down the street. I keep one foot in front of the other, slowly, slowly, and I'm nearly invisible.

CHAPTER 6

Getting across London when you haven't got no money isn't easy. I forgot to bring my travelcard. I creep in the back doors of the buses and throw a stink-eye at anyone who gives me a second glance. If the bus drivers notice, they don't say nothing. They just want a quiet shift. Me, I want a quiet body. You know when you drop a Mento in a bottle of Diet Coke and it all fizzes up and explodes? That's what it's like inside me right now.

I hold on to the seats in front to try to make myself steady. When I have to change buses, I almost cross the road and go back the way I came. But what's the point? When the foster carer finds out I'm missing, she's gonna call the police. If Kandi's dad sees me before I see Kandi, *he's* gonna call the police. Whatever happens, the police are gonna get called anyway, so I might as well carry on.

I get off the last bus and stand on the street where my sister lives. I didn't even have to look up the address. I've remembered it by heart. It's a long street. I could take another bus right down to Kandi's door, but any time soon my luck's gonna run out with the drivers.

So what's the plan, Chay Chay? You've come all this way to see your sister, so how are you gonna do it then?

It's past ten at night now. Even if it was midday, I couldn't just go and knock on that door. When Kandi's dad let me and her FaceTime, it couldn't be private. Every time I opened my mouth to say something to Kandi, I had to remember that her dad was sitting just out of sight. I always made sure I was knitting to keep me calm. Even so, last time I let out a swear word by mistake and that was the end of that. That man's gonna be so happy when I'm locked away. There ain't no video calls happening from prison.

I stop by an empty bus shelter. The light from it seems to shine through my head and make my thoughts glow. So what am I gonna say to Kandi?

Well, thanks to Blake, I'm never gonna send the letter I wrote earlier. Because, serious, Kandi's the only person I really need to say sorry to. We'd still be together if I could have held things down at school, didn't run off my mouth, if I'd damn well said sorry to the teachers when I was asked. But, man, I just need to see Kandi full stop. It's been so long.

I carry on walking. The road behind me is busy with traffic, but straight in front it's just houses and pavement and street lights.

Kandi's dad's house is at the end of a terrace with an alleyway and a gate. There's a street light by the front door. I just stay on the street thinking. Kandi's room must be at the back. She told me once how she looked out the window and saw three cats staring each other out in the middle of the garden. She called them Bananas, McDonald's and Skater Boi. Kandi said that if the cats came back, she'd try to take a picture of them for me so maybe I could knit them for her. I don't know if they ever did.

The light's on in the front room, but the curtains are drawn. I listen hard to see if there's a TV going, but I can't hear nothing. I also don't want to wait here too long. That's the secret. You have to be like Goldilocks's porridge and get it just right. Move too fast and folks are gonna notice. Don't move at all and folks are gonna notice. Always look like you know exactly where you've got to be and you know how to get there.

I walk towards the gate like I own it and push it. The gate opens. Man doesn't lock his gate? This is London! You don't make it easy for folks to come and thief your goods. Though Mum and me once lived in a ground-floor flat where the window frames were rotting away. The gap was so big we had to fill the space between the wood and the glass with a Pampers nappy – a clean one, of course. (It was good for catching the damp.) Anyone could have shoved the nappy away from outside, pushed their hand through the gap and opened the window. I suppose thieves reckoned that anyone who was blocking their window with a nappy didn't have much to take.

I step through the gate and walk down the side path to the back garden. The security light flashes on. I hold my breath and suddenly I'm seeing all the garden at once. There's a plastic table and chairs, pots of flowers and one of them oil-drum barbecues they have at Caribbean food stalls. I see that the bolt's rusted open on the inside of the gate. Then the security light flashes off. A bus goes past on the road in front. Even the bus engine ain't louder than my heart right now.

Nobody opens the back door or calls out of a window. Maybe the cats and the foxes set the light off all the time. I look up at the windows. One room has closed blinds. Another has curtains with a pale yellow glow leaking out between the edges. Kandi! That's her! That's the Barney the dinosaur night light I bought her when she was still little. Man, she's almost at big school and she's still got it.

Social workers and teachers and counsellors are always telling me that I've got choices. My choices right now are to turn around and leave my little sister's garden, or to wake her up and plunge myself in a massive pit of crap. While my brain's working this out, I'm already fumbling on the ground for a stone. Then I'm throwing it hard towards that yellow glow. It cracks against the glass and I almost regret this choice. The curtain sweeps aside and the window opens.

Kandi's dad stares down at me. I haven't got no flight and no fight neither. I seriously can't move.

"Who's down there?" he yells.

I realise that he can't see me. I need to wait until he leaves the bedroom, then make a run for it. *Please, body! Please! Help me get out of here!*

I see the cat just as it jumps over the neighbour's fence. It runs towards me and the security light flashes on. Me and the cat might as well be main stage at the O2.

"Charlene?" Kandi's dad yells. "Is that you? What the hell are you doing here?"

Kandi's dad is called Sheldon. I was once gonna knit a devil's face that looked like his, but I ran out of wool.

Sheldon was sorry he couldn't take me after Mum died. He said there was no room and he didn't know me that well anyway. They were together for a couple of years, but he never lived with us.

Sheldon could have got to know me better if he wanted to. I could have told him how I got in trouble in Year 7 at school because I got in late after I went to have a word with Kandi's teacher to make sure she had a place at breakfast club. Or how I helped Kandi with her reading and writing and took back her library books when she forgot. Or how me and her used to make up silly names for every cat we saw. All Sheldon had to do was ask me. I would have told him all that. He could have taken me too.

As I stand outside his house now, the window slams shut. I could run, but what's the point? Sheldon's seen me. Maybe, just maybe, he'll understand. Maybe he'll let me see my sister. If she's sleeping, he doesn't have to wake her up. *Please let me see her!*

The cat slinks away. The security light flashes off. I wait.

Kandi's dad switches on the light in the kitchen and it spills out into the garden. I've still got time. I could run, but the back door opens and Sheldon's standing there.

I wish he looked more like Kandi, then maybe I wouldn't feel so angry with him. But Aunty Jasmine says that Kandi looks like Mum and I look like my dad. She's right about Kandi. I've got no idea about me.

"What are you doing here?" Sheldon asks.

"Can't you guess?" I say.

Sheldon shakes his head. "Nuh. You're not seeing her."

"Why not?" I ask.

These aren't the words I want to say, but he's not asking me the right questions. He's not asking me nothing at all. Why doesn't he just say, "Why do you want to see her, Charlene?" Or, "How did you get here, Charlene?" Or, "Are you OK?" Then maybe I could tell him that I want to say sorry to my sister. Instead, it's like I'm plugged into the sun again and it's burning its way through me.

Sheldon says, "Because it's late."

"Even if it was early, you wouldn't let me," I reply.

"No, Charlene, I wouldn't and you know why."

"No I don't, *Sheldon*," I say. "Why don't you tell me?"

Sheldon's eyes narrow. "I'm done with you, Charlene. I don't want you anywhere near my girl."

He goes to close the door, but I lunge forward and shove it open again. "She's *my* sister!" I say.

"Get out of my house!" Sheldon shouts.

He pushes me and I fall back. The door slams shut and I can see him in the kitchen with his phone in his hand. I sit there feeling the cold stone of the path through my jeans. I know he's jabbing three numbers: 9 – 9 – 9.

I stand up slowly and brush down my jeans. Kandi's dad is talking on his phone, shooting looks through the window at me. I walk over to one of the flowerpots. It's supposed to have flowers but whatever was in there has died. But it's full of earth.

I pick the flowerpot up. It's proper heavy, not one of those plastic things. I walk towards the kitchen window. Sheldon's eyes open wide. He's walking back towards the door, still talking on his phone. I lift the pot above my head. Flakes of earth fall off the side into my hair. I don't care. I think of my sister upstairs in her room, so close to me. All Sheldon had to do was let me see her.

I heave the pot up over my head. All that hot-sun energy in my arms makes me move fast. The pot slams against the window and drops to the ground. Kandi's dad stares at me through the cracked glass.

"Chay Chay?" The voice comes from the window above. "What are you doing?"

I look up. Kandi's leaning out of her window. It's not just her. She's got two friends with her and one of them is crying so hard I can hear it in the garden.

CHAPTER 7

I run. I don't know why and I don't even know where I'm going. I've still got that energy. Man, fight or flight? I can do both at the same time now. I know the police are gonna come for me, but I don't even try to hide. Then suddenly I'm so tired I can hardly stand.

I sit on a wall by a church and take out my phone. I try to call Skye, but she isn't picking up. I start to tap out a message, but now I don't know what to say. I scroll through my numbers. A for Annie. I delete her from my contacts. I delete Bash too. Down through all my contacts until I come to Kandi.

It's her old number, I know, but I could never delete it. I need to see her name there.

Kandi … Man. I don't think I'm ever gonna forget her looking down on me like that. I shamed her in front of her friends. I shamed myself. Her dad must be calling social services right now, yelling at them for not keeping me away from her. *"Charlene's violent! I was scared for my daughter's safety!"* Sheldon's gonna show them the window and of course they're gonna agree. *"Yes, she is violent. We won't let her near her sister ever again."*

I hear a car engine and see the police car driving towards me. It slows down and stops. The car door opens and two of them get out. They say hello. I don't answer. I don't feel like friendly conversation.

They're both men, one mixed race, one white. The white one calls out my name. I don't know if they expect me to say, "Yes," like I'm in school registration. I still don't say nothing.

They walk towards me and ask me if I'm all right. I push my phone back into my pocket and they both touch those belts they wear, the ones that have their stuff hanging from them. The feds say that they need to talk to me about some damage to a property and some threatening behaviour.

I stand up. They ask me to stay calm even though I've kept my mouth shut. They get closer and closer and I want them to stop. They keep coming and I still don't move.

The feds stop walking. One of them is the same height as me. The other one's a bit shorter. They keep talking, using my first name like we've been friends since we were babies. I step towards them and they touch their belts again. The thing sticking out must be their taser or maybe a baton. What the hell do they think I'm gonna do? Turn into Captain Marvel and throw them harder than I threw the flowerpot? I carry on past them towards the car.

My head's full of Kandi again. That shame keeps burning inside me, but I'm angry too. If Kandi's dad had taken me as well, me and Kandi could still see each other. If Aunty Jasmine didn't have twins, me and Kandi could still see other. If Mum didn't die, me and Kandi would still be with each other. Man, I didn't cause none of this crap, but everything bad comes back to me.

I look behind me. The feds are right there, eyes on me, waiting for the badness to happen. Is that what they want? Man, I've got nothing to lose. If badness is gonna come back to me, I might as well make it mine in the first place. So I kick their car so damn hard I think I've broken a toe. I feel one of them touch my arm. I spin around and I kick him too.

CHAPTER 8

One thing that the police have got on those belts for sure is handcuffs. They snap round my wrists and I'm loaded into the car. Then I'm unloaded at a police station. And that's how I feel, like I'm the bag of dirty washing that no one wants to deal with.

I nod when the feds ask me if I'm Charlene Yewless. When they're happy they've got my details, they make me give them my phone and the two-pound coin that had fallen through the hole in my jacket pocket into the lining.

The feds check I don't need to see no one about my toe, then I'm taken down to the cell. Again. Maybe after a while you get used to it, but, man. I just want to puke again. I just want to lie on my face and pull the blanket over my head. I just sit there, pressing my fingers together and trying to empty my head of everything.

*

When they take me out of the cell it's to ask me more questions. They take more photos, more swabs, more fingerprints. Now they've got me twice.

It's a different appropriate adult, a different lawyer, a different fed interviewing me.

I nod and I say yes and no. I tell the fed that I just wanted to see my sister. I don't know why I kicked the car or the policeman. They say that the police officer I kicked has to have medical attention. Am I sorry about it? I know that kick hurt me more than him. My toe was already screaming at me after kicking the car. Trainers don't provide much barrier. The kick barely dented his trousers. But I don't answer the fed because I don't want to answer no more questions at all. I sit there with my arms crossed and let them all talk around me.

The policewoman leans forward so she knows I'm looking at her.

She says, "Are you close to your sister, Charlene?"

I almost tell her about the good times, when Mum was feeling all right. She'd let me and Kandi make play dough out of flour and food colouring, and hats out of cornflakes boxes, and paint a purple Kandisoraus on our bedroom wall. I taught Kandi how to play the *Lion King*'s "Circle of Life" on her recorder, though I reckon only I would have recognised Kandi's version. When Kandi laughed, it made me laugh too. I don't laugh in the same way now.

I just say to the policewoman, "Yeah. I suppose so."

I make a decision then. I'm not gonna talk about Kandi to no one else. I'm gonna keep all of her to myself because every time someone else mentions her name, it's like Kandi starts to disappear. I assaulted a police officer. I stabbed Blake with the knitting needle. It's gonna be a long time until I see Kandi again. I need to cling on to as much of her as I can.

*

Three weeks go by. I'm living in a home in Kent. It's like my life's been tied up in a sack made out of mammoth wool. It's thick and heavy and there ain't no gaps to let in daylight. Everything's going on around me, but I haven't got the energy to open the sack to look out at it.

I don't go back to a normal school. Social services send me to a pupil referral unit because they don't think local schools will "meet my needs". There's ten of us in the class and the teachers do their best. We have to pass English and Maths or we have to do the GCSEs again.

A couple of kids in my class have already been in prison and they make it sound like a party. Just as well I've met other kids who've been inside and tell me otherwise, or I might believe them. One of my classmates finds out that I kicked a fed and starts to big me up. They want me to give the teachers stress. I don't. But I don't answer my name. I don't do no homework. Everything feels so dark, I can only see a few things at a time. None of those things are English and Maths.

I'm still trying to keep Kandi in my head. I don't want her to start fading, like Mum. I've even got some photos of Mum. I can remember the big things like my sixth birthday party and when Mum brought baby Kandi back from the hospital. I can remember when Mum got angry and shouted and scared us. But it's harder to remember everyday things like what Mum would wear when she took us to school or what mug she liked for her tea. I haven't got no pictures of Kandi because her dad took the albums. I don't want her to disappear like Mum.

The other thought that fills up my head is that I'll have to go back to the police station. My stomach knots up when I think about it, which is all the time. I see the knitting needle stuck in Blake's skin and I want to throw up. I feel the shame that burned through me when I saw Kandi and her friends looking down from her window. I see my own foot as if it doesn't belong to me kicking the police car and the fed. And the string in the neck of that mammoth-wool sack I'm in gets pulled tighter and tighter. On the weekends, I don't come out of my room at all. I lie on my bed and let all those thoughts lie heavy in my head.

It's Saturday. I don't know what time it is, but it can't be too early. I can hear two of the younger kids outside in the garden chasing each other with water guns. There's a knock on my bedroom door and someone yells that there's a parcel been delivered for me.

I make myself get out of bed. There's a kid called Georgie here who likes to break into other folks' post. I'm not in the mood for an argument. I go down and collect the parcel. It's a cardboard box, maybe the size of one of them small suitcases on wheels. When I pick it up, it's lighter than I expect. I turn it over. When I see the return address on it, I think about giving the box to Georgie so he can mash it up. But then one of those knots in my stomach loosens a bit, because I think I know what's inside.

It's from Annie and she sure as hell knows how to wrap up something secure. Aliens could come and blast the Earth into pieces, but the tape on this box would stay stuck. It's like she's used two rolls of that brown shiny parcel tape and wrapped it round the whole thing twice. Then another time, just to be sure.

Then, finally, I can open it wide. Annie has sent packs of knitting needles, plastic ones, all sizes, and wool. So much wool! It's like she'd gone into a yarn shop and said, *"One of those, one of those and one of those, please."*

The wool's different colours and different thicknesses. I count three blues, a dark green like glass bottles, a thin shiny black with silver threads, some red. I spread it all out on the floor and touch the balls, one at a time. It's decent wool, not stuff from the bottom of a sale bin. I know it's gonna slide over my needles, so soft I hardly know it's there. Before I realise, there's a thread of baby blue wool between my fingers and thumb and I'm casting on. I don't know what I want to make and my fingers are all clumsy. But as I lay down the rows it's like that heavy sack I'm in opens a little bit and I can see some light.

When I finally put down my needles, I notice an envelope at the bottom of the box. I open it and there's a card from Annie. It has a dinosaur on the front – one of the flying ones that look like a duck got mixed up with a bat. Annie sent a whole load of other dinosaur pictures too. She says she's sorry about everything that happened and that this time the blanket will be even better.

Who am I knitting a blanket for? I want to yell. There's no point if I can't give it to Kandi myself.

Then at the bottom of the note Annie says that if social services agree, she'd love to see me again. And if I agree too.

I don't at first. It's been nearly a month since I left Annie's place. I can't forget the look she gave me when she was helping Blake out the door. Then I read her note again. *"Sorry about everything."* She's sorry. It's like Annie understands. I feel that heavy sack opening wider and the world gets more bright. I'm still not sure though.

I message Skye. She calls me. Skye's looking after her little cousin and they've got *Postman Pat* on in the background. I used to watch that with Kandi, though she preferred *Octonauts*. Skye reckons that maybe if I get Annie on my side, she might help me persuade the social workers to let me have contact with Kandi again. Right now, every letter has to be sent to Kandi's dad for him to decide whether to give it to Kandi. Man needn't bother lying. I know it's gonna go straight in the bin.

So I say yes to Annie. I don't tell Skye, but I liked Annie. And yeah, I kinda miss her too.

*

It takes another three weeks before Annie can come. My new social worker's off sick and there ain't no one around to make the decision.

It's like me and Annie live in different worlds now. When her car pulls up, I realise I'm blushing. I don't even blush when I meet up with some boy for the first time. Annie isn't wearing her yoga pants, but she's casual in jeans and a shirt. A couple of the other kids here come out to see her too. I never talk about myself, so they're pretty damn curious.

Annie's brought a picnic hamper. She says that after we've finished eating, I can use the basket for my wool. We drive half an hour through these windy country roads. It's a bit awkward because we don't know what to say to each other. So Annie concentrates on her driving and I play with my phone even though I'm feeling a bit sick with all the twisting and turning.

We end up at the seaside and that makes me smile. It's like the freshness is blowing the rest of the darkness away. The tide's right out, so we've got plenty of space to lay out our food. Except, it's like every seagull in the area has been on a call to his out-of-town mates inviting them over to feast. Man, we are mobbed by seagulls.

Annie made this cheese and potato pie special for me, but as soon as she cuts a slice, one of these gangster birds swoops down and snatches it off her plate. I read somewhere that chickens are really dinosaurs, but, man, anyone who's been close up to a seagull knows that these are the monsters.

We pack everything away, but we're laughing. Annie's asking me about where I'm living now and I tell her about all the other kids and then about school. She frowns then and says I should be in mainstream education. I've got so much potential, but I need it drawn out of me.

I don't say nothing to that. It wasn't like I was having loads of fun at the school I was at before. Then Annie tells me she heard that Charity got permanently excluded for throwing her shoe across the dining room. That makes me happy again.

We sit in a shelter and eat ice cream watching the seagulls divebombing the tourists for chips. Annie asks me what I'm knitting. I show her a picture on my phone. I don't know what it's gonna be, but it feels good. Then I take a deep breath and I ask her, "Will you help me see Kandi again?"

Annie doesn't say nothing. Ice cream drips down her cone to the ground.

"Of course I want to," Annie says.

Everything in me pulls tight. The ice-cream cone crunches as my hand grips it harder. There's gonna be a "but" ...

"But," Annie says, "there's a certain subject we've been ignoring today, isn't there, Charlene?"

Yes, Annie, there is. Your son deliberately upset me. He pulled apart my knitting and then called me a psycho in front of the police.

"Blake behaved badly," Annie says. "Very badly."

You're telling me? I damn well hope you told him that too.

"Of course I didn't witness the incident ..." Annie goes on.

But you saw the wool in his room, Annie. You know what he did. You know what it meant to me.

"So I can't say if you over-reacted or not," Annie adds.

Isn't that what you're saying now?

She turns to look at me and says, "I've persuaded Blake to take part in mediation. You and Blake have a meeting and there will be someone to help you sort things out. I spoke to a lawyer friend. He said that maybe ... well, a youth caution is the best option for you. For this, anyway. That would be the best thing." Annie gives me a sad smile. "But then you go and kick a policeman! But perhaps, if ..."

Annie looks at me.

"If you *could* do it ..." Annie says.

She's let her ice cream melt so much it's now dripping through the bottom of her cone. I'm still waiting for her to finish the sentence.

At last Annie says, "You have to say sorry to Blake, Charlene."

I stand up. She stays sitting.

"Charlene, I understand," Annie says. "You may not forgive Blake, but sometimes you have to play the game. Especially if you want to see Kandi again, you ..."

I walk away. Annie catches up with me.

"This is how the world works," she says. "I didn't make up the rules. I don't like the rules. But sometimes you have to play along."

"No!"

I never knew I could scream that loud. People stare at us. Annie glances around and tries to put a hand on my arm. I scream at her to get off. I tell Annie that she was always gonna take Blake's side. I'm shouting and crying and calling her names and then she backs away.

I walk off and all the people part to let me through. I walk down the steps across the pebbles to the edge of the sea. I keep on walking until I feel the sea seeping into my trainers and socks. I stand there until I can breathe properly again. After a while, I see that Annie's standing by my side. The water comes up past her ankles.

Annie says, "Shall I take you back?"

I nod.

CHAPTER 9

Click, click, click.

My knitting looks like a blue sky. It's not just one blue, it's all the blues. I know the sky's not just blue, so maybe later I'm gonna add some of the grey wool. I might put in some orange streaks too, like a sunset. I have to decide soon. The knitting's already half the size of my bed.

It was my birthday yesterday. I got a card and a gift voucher from Aunty Jasmine. She's moving to Coventry so the twins can be closer to their dad. The people in the home I'm staying in were gonna arrange a birthday tea for me, but I told them I wouldn't go. They bought me a cake anyway and Georgie sang "Happy Birthday" outside my bedroom door. I got a card from Annie, and Skye messaged me. I hoped Kandi would send a card. Maybe she did and her dad only pretended to post it.

And today I'm waiting for my new social worker to take me to the police station. I'm gonna find out what happens next. My fingers and thumbs are moving so fast with these needles. Maybe it's not just sky I'm knitting. Maybe it's water too.

Social services got me a lawyer called Shelley and we've already talked on the phone about what might happen today. She reckoned that Blake's hand would heal all right, though if it went to court, he might try to say otherwise. Shelley didn't mention no mediation. But even if Blake's hand got better, it didn't change the fact, Shelley said. I'd still stabbed it with a knitting needle. There would be consequences just for that. But now I could be looking at new charges: criminal damage and assaulting a police officer. If I was truly sorry, it might help our case, Shelley told me.

I didn't answer.

I think about what Annie said. She was right – it *is* easier to play the game. Can I make myself look shorter and a bit more delicate and a bit more white? Can I have the "sorries" dribbling out my mouth all over the place? I could do it if I really tried. And I do feel a bit sorry for the things I've done. But what's the point of even trying now? Even if I knit a sorry so big I can wrap it round the world, I'm never gonna see my sister again. And already … already … I think she's starting to fade.

*

When I get to the police station, me and Shelley talk in the side room first. She isn't how I imagined. She's Black and has got an afro. A short afro, but an afro. Shelley must think I'm rude because I'm staring. I always imagined that Black women got banned from doing important stuff unless they had hair that hung downwards.

The first thing Shelley says to me is, "How are you?"

She even leaves a space for me to answer – a proper answer. I just stare at her. I don't know how to tell her how I am.

Shelley says, "Is everything a bit overwhelming?"

I nod and breathe in hard, trying to suck my tears back into my body.

"Do you need a drink?"

"Some juice, please," I reply.

Shelley sticks her head out of the door. I hear her ask the social worker to buy me some juice from the newsagent's across the road.

"What we talk about here is just between you and me," Shelley says. "I don't tell the police. I don't work for the police. I just work for you."

I look at her.

"Do you believe me, Charlene?" Shelley asks.

I want to.

"I need to make sure that whatever happens today is the best thing for you," she adds.

I look away from her. Nothing can be "best".

Then Shelley starts to ask me questions. They're not about Blake – not at first. She asks me where I'm living and what it's like. She asks me if I see my family and my mouth runs away before I can stop it, telling her about Mum and Aunty Jasmine and Kandi. I say so much about

Kandi. It's like I stored her up inside me, but she's been pushing at the doors, waiting to burst out.

It's weird. The more I talk about Kandi, the brighter she becomes in my head. She stops fading. I talk even more – about how big Kandi was when she was a baby and how she was born with so much hair I could plait it from when she was two months old. How I used to mash avocado and banana together and feed her. How Kandi saw some kids' programme with dinosaurs and then that was it. She was obsessed with them.

Shelley puts down her pen. "She means everything to you."

It isn't a question. I don't need to answer. That's good, because no matter how hard I breathe in, I can't stop the crying. I don't make no noise. It's just tears mixed in with my make-up. Shelley hands me the box of tissues and says I can take as long as I like.

When I calm down, I tell Shelley how I knitted some daisies for Mum and they were left in the hospital. Aunty Jasmine found them and laid them on Mum's coffin at the church. After the service, Kandi's dad said he was taking the knitted daisies home with him. I thought he was taking me too.

Shelley sits back and looks at me.

She says, "Charlene, I'm so sorry that this happened to you."

"You're sorry?" I say.

"I am, Charlene. Very sorry."

I sit back too. Something unwinds inside me, twists out of me. I breathe in and it doesn't hurt.

"Thank you," I say. It's a whisper.

"Don't give up, Charlene," Shelley tells me. "I'm by your side. We will fight this together."

After that, we talk about Blake. Shelley wants to know everything that led up to it. She makes notes about the security guard and the make-up and Charity and the head teacher. Then Shelley puts down her pen again when I start talking about the dinosaur blanket. She doesn't say nothing at all. Then she starts asking me about what I've just said, making notes as I'm talking. She even lets me see the notes to check she's got it right.

My new social worker and Shelley come into the police interview room with me. I ask if I can bring my knitting. Shelley shows the police that the needles are plastic and can't hurt no one. They can't find no one to agree. I think they're scared of getting in trouble if I do something bad. In the end Shelley asks to speak to someone higher up and they allow it. As soon as I sit down, I take out the wool and needles.

Click, click, click.

It's like my hands have got their own brains and don't need me to think for them.

Shelley tries to tell the police that I shouldn't even be given a caution. Do they want to push another Black young person into the criminal justice system? she asks. Shelley says a caution's gonna go on my record and I might have to mention it in the future. Do they want to ruin my future?

I watch it all going back and forward. The police don't look impressed.

I knit faster. When they ask me about Blake, I make myself find the words and then keep the words soft even when I want to shout and cry. I tell them about my mum dying and Kandi living with her dad and the blanket I was knitting.

"Blake Morrisey purposely unravelled the present this child was knitting for her young sister," Shelley says. "It was an act of pure cruelty. And have we forgotten that Blake should not have been in my client's bedroom in the first place?"

The police nod. I see them glance at my new blanket. One of them says, "You take your knitting seriously, Charlene."

He doesn't even say it in a jokey voice. He sounds like he means it. I nod.

Click, click, click.

My blanket's flowing off my needles and onto the table.

When we come out of the police station, the sky is still blue. It's all the blues. Shelley shakes my hand and drives away. She said she'll be here next time.

*

So, what's gonna happen next? The police are still working out what to do about me kicking the fed. Shelley keeps in touch to keep me up to date. She's heard that the fed didn't even get a bruise from my kick. But I still kicked him. There will be punishment.

I got cautions for Blake and the window. There's gonna be a meeting with me and Blake if he agrees. Me and Shelley talked about it for a long time. I didn't want to meet him. Shelley said I had every right to be angry, but I did hurt him. She agreed that he hurt me in a different way. So in this meeting, both me and Blake have to say sorry. It's got to come from both sides. Shelley's also pushing for me to have a meeting with Kandi's dad. That really scares me, but if I want to rebuild my relationship with Kandi, that's where it starts.

When Shelley and I were leaving the police station, she said, "Kandi must miss you too, Charlene. I don't think Kandi's dad wants her to be unhappy. He just wants her to be safe. Do you understand?"

I nodded.

"Then you have something to prove to him," Shelley added.

I nodded again. The shame flared up and sizzled out.

Shelley told the police that I need to be referred to a counsellor too. Part of it's to stop me doing things I'll regret when I'm angry, but most of it's to talk about Mum – the good things and the things I don't want to remember.

I take out my knitting and hold it up. I know what it needs. It needs people. I have so much wool and suddenly my brain's full of ideas. I'm gonna knit me and Kandi and Mum and Aunty Jasmine and even my twin cousins. Maybe I'll put Annie and Shelley in there too. And there's plenty space for Skye. And one more thing? There's gonna be a brontosaurus, right in the front, its long neck snaking up past the trees towards the sun.

If you are a young person under 21 in custody and need advice, the Howard League run a free advice line: **0808 801 0308**